THE
TEDDY BEARS' PICNIC

Retold by STEVEN ANDERSON

Illustrated by TAKAKO FISHER

CANTATA
LEARNING

WWW.CANTATALEARNING.COM

CANTATA LEARNING

Published by Cantata Learning
1710 Roe Crest Drive
North Mankato, MN 56003
www.cantatalearning.com

Library of Congress Control Number: 2015932794
Anderson, Steven
    The Teddy Bears' Picnic / retold by Steven Anderson; Illustrated by Takako Fisher
    Series: Sing-along Animal Songs
    Audience: Ages: 3–8; Grades: PreK–3
    Summary: In this classic song, teddy bears come to life. And what do teddy bears
do when they come to life? They gather in the woods to have a hidden picnic, of
course!
    ISBN: 978-1-63290-370-9 (library binding/CD)
    ISBN: 978-1-63290-501-7 (paperback/CD)
    ISBN: 978-1-63290-531-4 (paperback)
    1. Stories in rhyme. 2. Bears—fiction. 3. Picnics—fiction.

Book design and art direction, Tim Palin Creative
Editorial direction, Flat Sole Studio
Music direction, Elizabeth Draper
Music arranged and produced by Musical Youth Productions

Printed in the United States of America in North Mankato, Minnesota.
122015   0326CGS16

ACCESS THE MUSIC!

SCAN CODE WITH MOBILE APP

CANTATALEARNING.COM

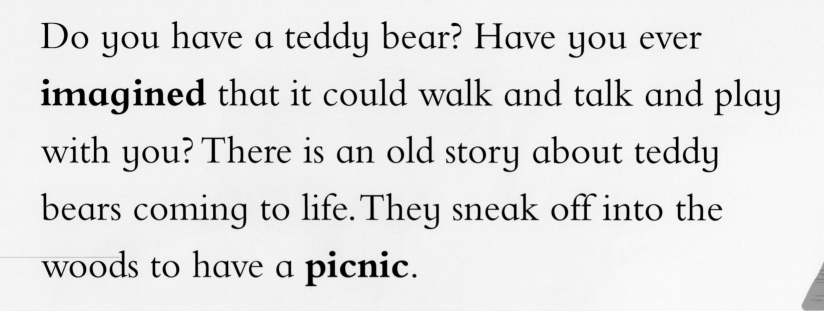

Do you have a teddy bear? Have you ever **imagined** that it could walk and talk and play with you? There is an old story about teddy bears coming to life. They sneak off into the woods to have a **picnic**.

To join in on their fun, turn the page and sing along!

If you go down to the woods today,
you're sure of a big surprise.

If you go down to the woods today,
you'd better go **in disguise**.

For every bear that ever there was
will gather there for **certain**,

because today's the day
the teddy bears have their picnic!

Picnic time for teddy bears!
The little teddy bears are having
a lovely time today.

Watch them, catch them **unaware**,
and see them picnic on their holiday.

Every teddy bear that's been good
is sure of a treat today.

There are lots of wonderful things to eat and wonderful games to play.

For every bear that ever there was
will gather there for certain,

because today's the day
the teddy bears have their picnic!

15

Picnic time for teddy bears!
The little teddy bears are having
a lovely time today.

Watch them, catch them unaware,
and see them picnic on their holiday.

For every bear that ever there was
will gather there for certain,

because today's the day
the teddy bears have their picnic!

At six o'clock their mommies and daddies
will take them home to bed.
They're tired little teddy bears.

Because today's the day
the teddy bears had their picnic.

SONG LYRICS
The Teddy Bears' Picnic

If you go down to the woods today,
you're sure of a big surprise.

If you go down to the woods today,
you'd better go in disguise.

For every bear that ever there was
will gather there for certain,
because today's the day
the teddy bears have their picnic!

Picnic time for teddy bears!
The little teddy bears are having
a lovely time today.

Watch them, catch them unaware,
and see them picnic on their holiday.

Every teddy bear that's been good
is sure of a treat today.

There are lots of wonderful things to eat
and wonderful games to play.

For every bear that ever there was
will gather there for certain,
because today's the day
the teddy bears have their picnic!

Picnic time for teddy bears!
The little teddy bears are having
a lovely time today.

Watch them, catch them unaware,
and see them picnic on their holiday.

For every bear that ever there was
will gather there for certain,
because today's the day
the teddy bears have their picnic!

At six o'clock their mommies and daddies
will take them home to bed.
They're tired little teddy bears.

Because today's the day
the teddy bears had their picnic.

The Teddy Bears' Picnic

Traditional Jazz
Musical Youth Productions

Verse

1. If you go down to the woods to-day, you're sure of a big sur-prise.

If you go down to the woods to-day, you'd bet-ter go in dis-guise.

Bridge

For ev-ry bear that ev-er there was will gath-er there for cer-tain, be-cause

to-day's the day the ted-dy bears have their pic - - nic!

Interlude

Pic - nic time for ted-dy bears! The lit-tle ted-dy bears are hav-ing a love-ly time to-day.

Watch them, catch them un-a-ware, and see them pic-nic on their hol-i-day.

Verse 2
Every teddy bear that's been good
is sure of a treat today.
There are lots of wonderful things to eat
and wonderful games to play.

Bridge

Interlude

Bridge

Outro

At six o'-clock their mom-mies and dad-dies will take them home to bed. They're tired lit-tle ted-dy bears.

(Much Slower)

Be-cause to-day's the day the ted-dy bears had their pic - nic.

ACCESS THE MUSIC!
SCAN CODE WITH MOBILE APP
CANTATALEARNING.COM

23

GLOSSARY

certain—sure that something will happen

imagined—used your imagination to think of something

in disguise—wearing a costume or clothes to hide who you are

picnic—a meal that is eaten outside, often at a park

unaware—not knowing something

GUIDED READING ACTIVITIES

1. The children are "in disguise." What does that mean? When might you put on a disguise?

2. Have you ever been on a picnic? Where did you go? What kinds of food did you eat? What activities did you do?

3. With a marker or crayon, draw a circle at the top of a piece of paper. Then add ears, eyes, and a round nose. Now make a larger oval under the circle. Add legs and arms. You just drew a teddy bear!

TO LEARN MORE

Hayes, Geoffrey. *Patrick in A Teddy Bear's Picnic and Other Stories*. New York: Toon Books, 2010.

Hissey, Jane. *Old Bear*. Plattsburgh, NY: Tundra Books, 2013.

Kelly, Luke. *Blanket & Bear, a Remarkable Pair*. New York: G. P. Putnam's Sons, 2013.

Meyers, Susan. *Bear in the Air*. New York: Abrams Books for Young Readers, 2010.